BEFORE THE STORM

BEFORE THE STORM

story by Jane Yolen

paintings by Georgia Pugh

Boyds Mills Press

Published by Caroline House
Boyds Mills Press, Inc.
A Highlights Company
815 Church Street
Honesdale, Pennsylvania 18431
Printed in Mexico

Publisher Cataloging-in-Publication Data
Yolen, Jane.
    Before the storm / story by Jane Yolen ; paintings by Georgia Pugh—1st ed.
[32]p. : col. ill. ;   cm.
Summary : A picture book that captures the still, languid moments before a summer storm.
ISBN 1-56397-240-9
1. Summer—Fiction—Juvenile literature. 2. Storms—Fiction—Juvenile literature. [1. Summer—Fiction.
2. Storms—Fiction.] I. Pugh, Georgia, ill. II. Title.
    [E]   1995   CIP
Library of Congress Catalog Card Number 94-70686

First edition, 1995
Book designed by Georgia Pugh
The text of this book is set in 21-point Perpetua.
The illustrations are done in oils.
Distributed by St. Martin's Press

10 9 8 7 6 5 4 3 2 1

el, my special next-door neighbor

—J. Y.

For Daniel, Adrien, and Hilary

—G. P.

It was a hot summer day,
the air crackling with heat,
and Strider lay panting by the barn door.
His tongue hung out of his mouth
like a big wad of pink bubble gum,
and the noise he made
was as snuffling as a train.

My brother, Pete,
was reading a book
about the frozen North.
My sister, Sara,
was coloring.
Each crayon grew soft and mushy
in her hand.

I just sat on the swing
in the chestnut tree.
It was too hot
even to consider swinging.

A squirrel ran in front of Strider,
then up a tree.
Strider raised one ear
and shifted his head slightly.
Then he closed his eyes.
It was *that* hot.

Mama stuck her head out of the door.
"Lemonade!" she called.
Only I got up,
my shorts leaving
a wet perspiration mark
on the swing seat.

The lemonade glass was cool in my hand.
I put it against my forehead.
That was almost better than drinking.
"Bring me some, too, Jordie,"
Sara called out.
"Me, too," Pete said,
never looking up from his book.
I got two more glasses
and held them against my cheeks.
I almost didn't want to give them up.

Then I went around the side of the house
where the hose lay curled
like a snakc in the short grass,
one end already tight around the faucet.
It was hard to do,
but I turned on the water
and held the hose as it uncurled
with the power of the flow.

Pop!
The water sprayed out,
catching me by surprise.
First it was hot,
from the hose lying all day in the sun.
And then it turned colder
than the frozen North in Pete's book.
I shivered.

Strider rose slowly to his feet,
shaking off lazy flies.
Then Sara came, flinging away her paper
and the last of the soft crayons.
Pete looked up from his book,
his eyes squinty from staring
over patches of deep snow.
"Me first!" he called. "I'm the oldest."

We took turns:
Pete running through the spray
like a runner winning a race.

Then Sara on her knees, laughing,
and shaking off the water
like Strider scattering flies.

When it was my turn in the spray,
Pete held it first low on my legs
like a strong waterfall,
then high on my head
like a gentle rain.
I looked up and let it patter down,
drinking until I was deliciously cold
inside and out.

When the real storm came
it surprised us all.
We ran screaming into the house,
leaving wet prints on the kitchen floor.

It rained all day long, with lightning,
and I watched the world cool down
until suddenly I found myself wishing
for the crackling heat and the hot summer sun.